# Aladdin
## and the Lamp

First published in 2006 by
Franklin Watts
338 Euston Road
London
NW1 3BH

Franklin Watts Australia
Hachette Children's Books
Level 17/207 Kent Street
Sydney
NSW 2000

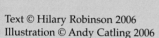
Text © Hilary Robinson 2006
Illustration © Andy Catling 2006

A CIP catalogue record for this book is available
from the British Library.

ISBN (10) 0 7496 6678 1 (hbk)
ISBN (13) 978-0-7496-6678-1 (hbk)
ISBN (10) 0 7496 6692 7 (pbk)
ISBN (13) 978-0-7496-6692-7 (pbk)

**Series Editor:** Jackie Hamley
**Series Advisor:** Dr Barrie Wade
**Series Designer:** Peter Scoulding

Printed in China

# Aladdin
## and the Lamp

by Hilary Robinson and Andy Catling

## W
### FRANKLIN WATTS
LONDON•SYDNEY

There once lived a poor, lazy
boy who only liked playing.
His name was Aladdin.

One day, a stranger appeared.
He was a magician. "I am
your uncle," he told Aladdin.
"Tell your mother I am here!"

Over supper, Aladdin's mother cried.
"Aladdin is so lazy," she said. "We
have no money since his father
died." The magician agreed to help.

Next day, the magician led
Aladdin up into the mountains.
They stopped to light a fire.

The magician threw some powder
onto the fire and chanted magical
words. Suddenly, the earth shook.

Then Aladdin saw a heavy stone with a brass ring. "Under this stone lies treasure," said the magician.

"To lift it, you must chant the names
of your father and grandfather."
Aladdin did as he was told.

Under the stone, Aladdin saw
long, winding steps. "Fetch me
the lamp in the cave. Wear
this ring," said the magician.

Aladdin walked through three
halls filled with treasure ...

... and a garden of fruit trees.
There, at the end of the garden,
was the lamp.

Aladdin took it and ran back
to the mouth of the cave.

"Give me the lamp!" shouted the magician. "Not until you get me out of here!" shouted back Aladdin.

The magician got angry. He threw
more powder onto the fire and the
stone rolled back.

Aladdin was trapped and scared.
He knew now that the man was
not his uncle, but a cunning
magician. "Why does he want
this old lamp?" thought Aladdin.

19

Aladdin twisted the ring on his finger. At once a genie rose up!

"I am the Genie of the Ring and will obey you in all things," he said.

"Please, get me out of here!" begged Aladdin.

Suddenly, the earth opened and the genie disappeared. Aladdin quickly escaped.

At home, his mother hugged him.
"Let me sell some cotton," she
said. "We need money for food."

"No, you will get more money
if you sell this old lamp,"
said Aladdin.

As Aladdin's mother cleaned the lamp, another genie appeared! "Your wish is my command, master," said the genie.

26

"Ermm, could you please bring us some food?" asked Aladdin.

The genie returned with four
silver plates laden with food.

He also granted lots of

other wishes for Aladdin!

And from that day on, the genie made sure that Aladdin and his mother were never in need again.

Hopscotch has been specially designed to fit the requirements of the National Literacy Strategy. It offers real books by top authors and illustrators for children developing their reading skills. There are 37 Hopscotch stories to choose from:

**Marvin, the Blue Pig**
ISBN 0 7496 4619 5

**Plip and Plop**
ISBN 0 7496 4620 9

**The Queen's Dragon**
ISBN 0 7496 4618 7

**Flora McQuack**
ISBN 0 7496 4621 7

**Willie the Whale**
ISBN 0 7496 4623 3

**Naughty Nancy**
ISBN 0 7496 4622 5

**Run!**
ISBN 0 7496 4705 1

**The Playground Snake**
ISBN 0 7496 4706 X

**"Sausages!"**
ISBN 0 7496 4707 8

**The Truth about Hansel and Gretel**
ISBN 0 7496 4708 6

**Pippin's Big Jump**
ISBN 0 7496 4710 8

**Whose Birthday Is It?**
ISBN 0 7496 4709 4

**The Princess and the Frog**
ISBN 0 7496 5129 6

**Flynn Flies High**
ISBN 0 7496 5130 X

**Clever Cat**
ISBN 0 7496 5131 8

**Moo!**
ISBN 0 7496 5332 9

**Izzie's Idea**
ISBN 0 7496 5334 5

**Roly-poly Rice Ball**
ISBN 0 7496 5333 7

**I Can't Stand It!**
ISBN 0 7496 5765 0

**Cockerel's Big Egg**
ISBN 0 7496 5767 7

**How to Teach a Dragon Manners**
ISBN 0 7496 5873 8

**The Truth about those Billy Goats**
ISBN 0 7496 5766 9

**Marlowe's Mum and the Tree House**
ISBN 0 7496 5874 6

**Bear in Town**
ISBN 0 7496 5875 4

**The Best Den Ever**
ISBN 0 7496 5876 2

**ADVENTURE STORIES**

**Aladdin and the Lamp**
ISBN 0 7496 6678 1 *
ISBN 0 7496 6692 7

**Blackbeard the Pirate**
ISBN 0 7496 6676 5 *
ISBN 0 7496 6690 0

**George and the Dragon**
ISBN 0 7496 6677 3 *
ISBN 0 7496 6691 9

**Jack the Giant-Killer**
ISBN 0 7496 6680 3 *
ISBN 0 7496 6693 5

**KING ARTHUR STORIES**

**1. The Sword in the Stone**
ISBN 0 7496 6681 1 *
ISBN 0 7496 6694 3

**2. Arthur the King**
ISBN 0 7496 6683 8 *
ISBN 0 7496 6695 1

**3. The Round Table**
ISBN 0 7496 6684 6 *
ISBN 0 7496 6697 8

**4. Sir Lancelot and the Ice Castle**
ISBN 0 7496 6685 4 *
ISBN 0 7496 6698 6

**ROBIN HOOD STORIES**

**Robin and the Knight**
ISBN 0 7496 6686 2 *
ISBN 0 7496 6699 4

**Robin and the Monk**
ISBN 0 7496 6687 0 *
ISBN 0 7496 6700 1

**Robin and the Friar**
ISBN 0 7496 6688 9 *
ISBN 0 7496 6702 8

**Robin and the Silver Arrow**
ISBN 0 7496 6689 7 *
ISBN 0 7496 6703 6

* hardback